I0755974

FINISHING LINE PRESS
www.finishinglinepress.com

On Queer Homesteading

essay by

Lindsey Danis

Finishing Line Press
Georgetown, Kentucky

On Queer Homesteading

ISBN 979-8-89990-419-6 First Edition

ACKNOWLEDGMENTS

"The Farmhouse" previously appeared in *Santa Fe Writers Project*

Publisher: Leah Huete de Maines
Editor: Christen Kincaid
Cover Art: "Queer Homesteading in the Hudson Valley," by Portia Apple Melita
Author Photo: Kristopher Johnson
Cover Design: Elizabeth Maines McCleavy

Order online: www.finishinglinepress.com
also available on amazon.com

Author inquiries and mail orders:
Finishing Line Press
PO Box 1626
Georgetown, Kentucky 40324
USA

Contents

To queer and trans people seeking community, building community and showing up for one another with grit and creativity

Historically queer histories get erased. If we want to preserve our history, we need to document it ourselves. -Cyril

Queer Erasure

When I came out at eighteen, I didn't know how to be gay. I'd never really known how to be straight, in hindsight, but now I could stop pretending. I grabbed at crumbs of queer culture—James Baldwin and Jeanette Winterson, *Paris is Burning* and *But I'm a Cheerleader*—and made a place for myself.

Years later, I volunteered at an LGBTQ+ archive in Boston's gay neighborhood, the South End. The archive was in a brownstone, above an AIDS soup kitchen, down the hall from the Bisexual Resource Center, around the corner from a gay bar my friends and I used to frequent. The archivist put me in charge of a file cabinet of ephemera: old newspaper clippings, flyers, magazines, directories, xeroxed newsletters and other paper scraps from the 1950s to present day, though the collection thinned in the early 2000s when we began to share information digitally.

It wasn't until the archives that I considered the lack of queer representation—decades of unvoiced stories—and how this erasure had complicated our quests to form identities and build relationships.

In Massachusetts, gay marriage had been legal for close to a decade. While we didn't have the same rights and responsibilities as the general population, it seemed possible to imagine a time when equality would extend to more than marriage. I wanted broader freedoms. I worried that widespread acceptance would dilute the bonds of queer community. For so long, we'd had only each other. What would it mean to be like everyone else, I wondered, on afternoons spent sorting through back issues of gay magazines.

Cities had long been positioned as the center of queer life. They were the antidote to confining suburban and rural existences, the places we could go and finally be ourselves. As equality advanced, urban queer life became blasé. Gayborhoods were dismantled by gentrification and assimilation. Flirtation was reduced to Grindr messaging. Gay bars closed, friends married or moved away, and I got married, too. Queer community became a pop-up affair, recreated with the occasional bar night or potluck supper. By the time I left Boston for the Hudson Valley, seeking access to nature and improved mental health, there wasn't much to lose.

In the Hudson Valley, a pretty agricultural area between Albany and New York City, gay bars and queer-inclusive service providers were spread out across an isolating geography of rivers and mountains. Roadside signs reminded us not to get comfortable in Trump's America. If we wanted queer community, we had to seek it out, mining social media, local magazines, and community boards for breadcrumbs of queer happenings. It reminded me of the archives; all those times we'd had to go in search of one another. How sweet it must have felt to discover the gathering spaces.

In oral history interviews, I spoke with other Hudson Valley LGBTQ+ people on the ways we build homes and cultivate community. Coming together in nature, could we heal the wounds of belonging queer people carried? Honoring our queer ancestors and finding common ground despite our differences, could we bloom in the very places we'd been told to leave?

Women's Land

Rural queer community has ancestry in the women's land communities that flourished in the 1970s. These sprang from radical feminism, which believed sex was the root of women's oppression. Radical feminists did not believe liberation was possible in a patriarchal society; freedom and equality were only possible with separation. Separatists called their spaces wimmin's land or womyn's land, quite literally taking 'men' out of the picture. Land communities bore names like A Woman's Place, WomanShare, Cloudland, Rainbow's End, hinting at an idealized union with nature.

Women's land communities were one part anarchist, one part collective organized by skill sharing and mutual aid. Women built shelter, grew and prepared food, cared for children, and earned money through cottage industries. Everything was shared.

In reality, the picture was less rosy. Women lived in poverty on marginal land. They struggled to learn the homesteading skills necessary for self-sufficiency. Member loss "was such a problem that fruiting shrubs planted on one particular land one year could not be located the next due to 100 percent membership turnover," wrote Sine Anahita in a doctoral study on these movements.

Some women moved to new collectives. Others ditched the movement outright. Over time, the women's land movement became majority lesbian. Unsurprisingly, those most deeply committed to separatism were those who didn't consider it a loss to go without men.

By the 1980s, directories united the network of land-based communities. Conferences provided networking opportunities, skills development, and a social scene. Collective publications filled with poems and stories that idealized country life and feminist values.

The 1980s were the golden age for women's land communities, though I imagine participants were too preoccupied with daily necessities to realize it. Farming was heavy labor, challenging in the best of conditions. Communities were isolated, with ramshackle housing and few creature comforts. Dismantling the patriarchy turned out to be harder than anticipated. Personal politics and infighting took a toll on committed activists. Bi and trans women felt excluded, as did BIPOC women, who left to create their own land communities. By the 1990s, women's land was largely replaced by a gentler form of community, the gayborhood.

When I first learned about lesbian separatists, I laughed. I wasn't able to appreciate the ways women's lives had been prescribed by men to the extent that married women needed their husband to co-sign their credit card application and unmarried women could be turned down outright. I couldn't understand how land could be a liberation tool.

Amy, a New Paltz-based activist I interviewed for my oral history project, understood the connection between land and liberation through her work in activism and permaculture.

After a near-death experience at age 59, Amy woke up to the urgency of living authentically. She felt an urge to "travel on my own and get away from everybody who knows me." She trekked to the jungles of Costa Rica, then drove across the country in a camper van on a self-discovery quest that culminated in coming out as a lesbian and divorcing her husband.

"Every single day writing in my journal I'm like, 'I know what I am, who I am,' and…it was like the people in my life weren't holding me as they wanted me to be. I had to look within and I knew it. My entire life I've been surrounded by lesbians who were just waiting for me to come out," Amy said. "I was born this way, but I was so busy working, I focused on the planet and all the things I wanted to do. I am a mother. So…I didn't admit it to myself until I was 59."

Now 63, Amy was dating for the first time in forty years, meeting women on Match.com and through the activist group OLOC, Older Lesbians Organizing for Change.

A committed permaculture gardener, Amy dreamed of opening her home to lesbians to live communally. Newly discovering herself after decades of opposite-sex marriage, Amy hoped homesteading with other lesbians would allow her to be seen and held in authenticity. As it did for the separatists, Amy's lesbian homesteading dreams offered the chance to build skills and broaden horizons within an intentional community.

Our conversation turned to the mundane challenges of homesteading: weeks of rain broken up by punishing ninety-degree days, the tick-borne diseases so common in our region. I described my latest garden plague, the invasive jumping worm, and Amy offered suggestions.

There were always bad years and plant pests and punishing weather, there was always a shortage of time and labor. In the summer of 2021, pandemic restrictions, collective fears, and ambiguous loss were unspoken additions to our litany of complaints.

Pre-pandemic, a local LGBTQ+ center had offered entry points into queer community, hosting monthly dinners, Latin dancing, and queer yoga. Now, the LGBTQ+ center had gone dark. June came and went without Pride parades. We had only Zoom and the occasional outdoor meetup to sustain connection. Trading gardening woes with Amy reminded me: this too was temporary.

The pandemic would end.

We would gather again.

We would gather differently.

The Carriage House

I grew up in a carriage house halfway between Boston, where my mother went to law school, and the South Shore suburb where my father worked. The house was in foreclosure when my parents bought it: 2,200 square feet set on a ⅓-acre lot.

Once it had been part of a big estate, surrounded by apple and pear orchards. This information I gleaned from a map that lived on a closet shelf in a spare bedroom. Where the pear trees had grown, one block over, was my best friend's house. There had been a fire and the main house burned, I was told, but this didn't explain what had happened to the pear orchards. I would stare at the map of the carriage house and its environment, as if careful study would fill in the missing pieces. What happened to the main house and its people?

On rainy days, my best friend and I would wander room to room knocking on wood panels, our ears pressed to the glossy molding. We were convinced the carriage house had secret passageways.

My parents separated when I was six. My father remarried one year later and had two kids. My mother had only me. We didn't need a five bedroom house for two people, but we stayed in the carriage house until I went to college. Every room had its own purpose: the guest bedroom where our neighbors lived while they renovated their kitchen, the laundry room, the computer room, and the junk room, filled with boxes of things we didn't use.

When I left for Vassar, my mother sold the carriage house and moved to Boston. The map was left behind for the new owners to discover.

Looking for hidden passageways and secret rooms was a way to frame my origin story differently. I'd been a shy kid, always with my head in a book, privately longing to be included.

I didn't feel a connection in my town or with my peers. My family fractured when I was young. The few memories I had of us all together were unhappy ones: slammed doors, arguments over who would get what, a yellow moving truck in the driveway.

I wanted another frame of reference, hoped my house's rich history might provide it. By reshaping my relationship to my environment, I could skirt around my family's dissolution and replace it with another line of ancestry.

The Farmhouse

My wife and I looked at over fifty houses in the Hudson Valley before we found the farmhouse.

It had good bones, but we'd had to overlook the owner's hoarder tendencies and cat obsession—there were cat shower hooks and cat hand towels, cat fly swatters and cat knick-knacks; ascending the hall stairs, where other people put family photos, were portraits of long-deceased cats.

Visiting with a real estate agent, I stood in the backyard and considered the property. If I went back inside, I'd have a crisis of faith over the overstuffed furniture that blocked the natural light and gave the house a cave-like atmosphere. Here in the yard, the place had an aura of rightness. We'd declutter and turn the summer kitchen, where the owner stored her antiques, into a writer's shed for me. We'd put in a big garden. We'd make the place ours.

"I hope you'll be as happy here as I was," said the woman who sold us the farmhouse. She'd raised three children, buried her husband, and now was moving to Buffalo to be closer to family. She gave us parting gifts: hand towels, French-milled soap, a framed photograph of the house and its original owners. Years ago, someone had sent it to her in the mail.

"This belongs with the house," she said, pressing the wooden frame into my wife's hands.

The sepia image showed the farmhouse as it had been in 1836, and the first family to call it home. The husband wore dark pants and a shirt with a button-down vest. His wife wore a long dark dress with puffy sleeves, corseted at the waist. An older child stood to her mother's shoulders, dressed to match. Off to one side was a nanny with a baby. The couple seemed ageless and unsmiling. They were younger than we were now, in our early thirties.

Behind them was the house: a two-story brick home with a Y-shaped chimney at the south end. The chimney had since been removed, but the exterior wall bore scars. The photo was taken in late fall or early spring or possibly winter, though no one wore coats. The trees that dotted the front lawn were bare-branched saplings.

Now, those saplings were 100-foot-tall black walnut trees whose mossy branches grew wood ear mushrooms. After rains, bits of bricks sometimes turned up in the yard stamped with REYNOLDS, the name of a local brickmaker. Digging a garden bed, we uncovered clam shells, glass bottles, and bits of scrap metal from a long-ago garbage heap.

As in the carriage house, time seemed to flow backwards and forwards. The present hummed with a connection to earlier times, sometimes quite literally.

While cleaning and painting the walls, shortly after we moved in, I heard Big Band music. We didn't have a radio. Our neighbors weren't playing music. It was November, a time when the veil between worlds was thin. House ghosts were making their presence known to us, I decided. As we settled in, the ghost radio quieted down. The spirits were happy with us; they appreciated our care for the house.

Our town was old enough to have its own municipal history book from the Images of America series. We requested it from the library and paged through, finding a photo of our house. A caption added these details: *Nearly adjacent to the tiny VanAken cottage is this wonderful brick home. This was the homestead of the Isaac and Serena Freer family. Isaac was a highway superintendent. This is the second Freer house of several on Main Street. The tall chimney rises from the kitchen wing.*

Another photo gave the names of the Freer's two children. Elsie was the oldest, her unruly brown hair tied back with a ribbon. The baby, Ruth, eventually settled in the family homestead with her husband, John DuBois.

Although the Freers were long dead strangers, I felt a connection to them. We tended the house they'd built. We gathered nuts from the black walnut trees they'd planted. The nuts were edible but impossible to open; a neighbor recommended we run them over with the car to crack the shell. Black walnut trees didn't bear nuts for twenty years and couldn't be harvested for wood for sixty; they were planted by grandparents for grandchildren. Now, they were our dubious heirlooms. We loaded them into wheelbarrows and dumped them into the woods for squirrels.

In the small gated cemetery behind the Dutch Reformed

Church, I searched for traces of Isaac and Serena, but there were too many Freers to determine which headstones were theirs. They were buried here, surrounded by family. They didn't need us to remember them. We hung the Freer family photo on a living room wall, finding space for them in our lives.

While the farmhouse could be restored to its former appearance with relative ease—strip off the front porch and back deck, rebuild the fireplace—my wife and I were the incongruous ones. We'd replaced the traditional farm family with a queer family in which we referred to our pets as our children.

"I think homesteading is about making and maintaining a space that's livable, and part of queerness is also making and maintaining a space for us to be alive in and to stay alive in," said Lydia, who identifies as a queer bi pan cis woman. Lydia owned a metaphysical shop by the Kingston waterfront.

When we spoke over Zoom, Lydia was at home alone. Set on a lake in Rosendale, Lydia's house was a folk Victorian that had been sold as a kit house in the 1870s or 1880s. "This particular house, I've seen it everywhere. I've seen it in Alligerville, I've seen it in Midtown Kingston, in High Falls, Cottekill. It's just a shape," she explained, though at the time of our interview, it had come to mean more than that. Her wife had initiated divorce. Lydia had fought to keep the house.

I thought back to my childhood, when my parents fought about the division of assets. There'd been a blue velvet armchair my father had wanted. When he tried to take it, I wailed. It was the perfect size for six-year-old me. I distilled my pain and anger over my parents' separation into the battle to keep the chair. My mother and I kept it, but I don't remember ever sitting there.

"I have definitely worked to create and build a home and then a small business in the area just to stay here and create a space for me. I feel really great when I'm able to welcome others into that space," Lydia said. With her shop, she'd worked hard to open a space that was actively "supportive or liberatory" for queer people.

If queerness was expressing our full selves or self-actualizing in a world that tried to box us in, connection required we strip away layers of protection that guarded against transphobia and homophobia. Like taking down old wallpaper, we exposed hidden parts of ourselves to new light. This level of vulnerability required trusting others to hold us as we wanted to be held.

Good Neighbors

My country neighbor introduced himself the day we moved in by letting himself in the back door with a spare key. He helped the previous owner with yard work and wanted to check out the new people.

Another neighbor left a coffee cake on our front steps. It was the sort of gesture we assumed belonged to previous generations.

Their warm welcome caught me off guard. In Boston, I'd been street harassed for being queer. Here, people waved from their cars as we walked our dogs. They stopped to ask what we were planting in our front-yard garden. I hadn't dared imagine rural neighbors would go out of their way to be kind.

When new people moved in, we left cookies at their door, paying forward the welcome we received. To be a good neighbor, I had to open myself up to living alongside—and in community with—people from different walks of life.

Turning toward neighbors was a small form of expanding our attention outward, of creating community bonds by giving time and resources to those outside the nuclear family. When I thought about connecting to queer community—how we showed up for others, and how fraught this often was for those of us who carried legacies of rejection or, as with my father, conditional acceptance—I thought of the graciousness my country neighbors showed me.

While modern homesteaders were more individualistic than the communes and cooperatives of the 1970s, we shared an urge to connect with something larger than ourselves: land, people, the historical past that inspired our self-sufficiency quests, symbolized by pioneer-era icons like Laura Ingalls Wilder.

Solitude was part of the appeal, but homesteading could not be done in isolation. It required many hands on deck, whether you were putting up a barn or putting up a harvest. To create a home that met our needs required skills and growth beyond our comfort zone. We were at once independent and in relationship with others, building community by how we showed up for ourselves and one another. For queer people, this was healing work.

The Garden

Cleaning, painting, renovating a dated bathroom: settling in felt like a game of house. It wasn't until I put in a front-yard garden, in 2016, that the farmhouse began to feel like home.

We'd grown plants before, but we weren't sure how to work with the black walnut trees, garden nemeses that poison other plants with 'acid rain' from the juglone found in the tree's roots, branches, leaves, pollen, and nuts.

We measured fifty feet from the tree canopy, the recommended safe zone from juglone, and staked out a raised bed. Over the next two years, one bed grew to six that stretched across our front lawn.

At gardening talks and plant swaps, my wife and I were often the youngest people. We traded our surplus ferns and hostas for ornamental grasses and brown-eyes Susans. We showed up, over and over, to learn how to garden better. Local gardeners provided inspiration and advice. Even if we were doing all the work ourselves, it didn't feel like we were alone.

In everyday life, I rushed from one deadline to the next. In the garden, time expanded. I harvested yellow pear tomatoes and red Thai chilies. I watched monarch butterflies touch down on zinnias. Overnight, mice nibbled on sunflower seeds and left a trail of droppings behind.

The garden wasn't easy, between the towering black walnuts and the deer who leaned over the fence to nibble plants, but it was mine. To solve its problems, I had to think creatively, try things that might not work, and be willing to try again. This was relationship work, and it made me rethink my relationships with ancestors.

My grandmother, Chessie, asked my mom and her sister to choose sides when my grandfather left her. My mother resented this and pulled back. When my mother was pregnant with me, she tried to reconcile. Chessie crocheted me a baby blanket, which sits in my mother's attic. She visited a few times, but things soured when I was an infant.

I knew her only from photos. Sometimes she would send birthday cards signed "Love, Chessie" or else "Love, Nana."

The cards were generic, her handwriting unfamiliar. There was never a kind note or a check like in the cards my *real* Nana sent.

When I was twelve, my mother drove me to the town where she grew up to meet Chessie for lunch. Chessie ordered fish and rice; I had fish and chips. She was dressed up with costume jewelry and dark lipstick, but her hands shook from years of drinking. Chessie was an alcoholic; this was why she wasn't part of our lives.

I imagined Chessie visiting a liquor store on the pretext of giving a party. She'd buy several bottles of gallon wine or cheap vodka. At another store, she would repeat the process. Then she would sit in a ranch house on a tree-lined suburban cul-de-sac, surrounded by cats and dogs she was too ill to care for, and drink.

I got this image of the alcoholic from pop culture, rounded out with bits of overheard conversation between my mom and her younger sister. I never pictured Chessie's hands writing my name on the birthday card and hesitating over the word love. I never thought about the act of licking the envelope to seal it or depositing the card in a mailbox. I never considered writing back. How could she love someone she didn't know? By extension, how could I?

When I was fourteen, Chessie died. My aunt and uncle cleaned out her house. Chessie's antiques, knick-knacks, clothes, and costume jewelry came to our house, alongside boxes of family photos. In grainy images, Chessie grinned with a devil-may-care smile, on the arm of a handsome soldier. Model pretty with a slim waist and wavy red-brown hair, she could have been anything, but she met my grandfather at a military dance and ran off with him. Her parents didn't approve of the relationship and cut ties.

By the time my grandfather left her, my mother was in college and my aunt was sneaking out of the house to party. Once my aunt moved away, Chessie had no one. When she died, the animals she kept for company were so neglected, they had to be euthanized.

I'd reduced Chessie to a trope. That was harmful. For a writer, it was lazy. Chessie had been more than a drinker. She played bridge and liked to garden; we had something in common. She would never have grown vegetables because my grandfather refused to eat them. Flowers, then: fragrant roses or hardy annuals as fiery as her hair.

While I gardened, I imagined alternative lives for my grandmother. What if she established a career, met someone new, found solace in the places women gathered—hair salons, card tables, garden clubs? What if she'd found healing? What if I'd called to say thank you for those cards, and we'd made time to know one another?

In late summer, gladiolus bloomed along the garden fence in yellows, oranges, and reds. My mother had planted them in her garden. As a kid, I'd marveled at the tall stalks of vibrant blooms. Now, they were a way of bringing the magic of my childhood home into my adult life, and of honoring all the people I'd been, who I was now, and who I might yet become.

In my early adulthood, a not-quite-nomadic existence, switching coasts, cities and apartments, was comforting. The constant change mirrored my upbringing, trading homes as dictated by a custody schedule. Staying in one place and allowing all parts of me to be seen was more unsettling. Homesteading was a chance to reparent myself, to build a home base where I would always belong.

From that growing sense of safety, I reached one hand back, to root Chessie's wayward soul. My attention couldn't soothe the pain of her disconnection and rootlessness, but my house had room for ghosts. She could stay if she wanted.

With the other hand, I cut my father out of my life. His love for me had always been conditional. Ever a dutiful daughter, I'd spent decades contorting myself into someone who might please him. I'd exhausted myself trying to become someone he would love. Queer community taught me that I was enough the way I was, that there was nothing selfish about being yourself.

Chosen Family

Paris is Burning chronicles Black and Latine performers in the Harlem ball circuit in the mid-to-late 1980s. The cult queer classic is a snapshot of a community ravaged not only by AIDS but by racism, poverty, homophobia, and transphobia. Despite these intersectional barriers, the documentary is a love song to old New York, and to queer joy.

Borrowing matrilineal kinship roles of mothers, aunts, and siblings, drag ball participants assembled into Houses that provided shelter, drag mentorship, and the nurturance many performers did not receive from biological families.

Armistead Maupin called these non-kinship groups our logical families, evoking the hero's journey when he wrote that all queer people must "join the diaspora" and venture beyond our families of origin to find the ones that "make sense for us."

Queer chosen families offered protection from a world that put conditions on our acceptance. Their structure mimicked the mutual aid support of women's land communities. Chosen families helped us overcome isolation, loneliness, and biological family rejection; they filled our unmet needs for intimacy in all its forms.

In our chosen families, we were fully seen, we were sheltered from homophobia and transphobia, we remembered those lost, and we dreamed of bright futures.

Things were better now than they used to be, but queer people of all ages continued to live with trauma, with trans and BIPOC LGBTQ+ populations experiencing a disproportionate share. According to the Trevor Project's 2022 survey, over 60 percent of LGBTQ+ youth said their homes were not affirming, and two in five reported their communities were not affirming.

There was a correlation between the violence queer people experienced, including the low-grade, persistent threat of harassment we came to expect as we moved through the world, and our mental well-being. The recent increase in anti-queer and anti-trans legislation was a reminder that our welcome and safety were contingent on others' comfort with our identities. Against the uncertain world, our chosen families provided a buffer.

For a long time, gay bars were our safe spaces—the only places queer people could be ourselves, publicly. As we gained broader societal acceptance, we lost many of the rituals and places that connected us. Pride started as a riot and became a corporate party. Assimilation and hookup apps transformed any bar into a queer bar. Gayborhoods gentrified, and queer people were priced out of the communities we built.

Pandemic restrictions accelerated the loss of queer spaces. In the 1980s, there were two hundred lesbian bars; by 2021, there were twenty-one. The Hudson Valley LGBTQ+ Center shut its doors in 2020 and has never resumed the level of programming it had before. The only nightclub in town, an inclusive space with a dedicated queer night, was sold to a New York City developer. The bartender who hosted queer parties quit the hospitality industry. The spaces we loved and lost joined the archive of queer spaces.

Connection in late-stage capitalism felt hollow, a box to check with a text message or Instagram like. Social media promised anytime engagement yet I'd never felt more distant from friends and loved ones. The binary of connected or disconnected overlooked the way community was built through small connections over time. Through asking for help, sharing wisdom or resources, and showing up for those around you.

Marcel and Cyril, a pansexual married couple living in Orange County, New York, had been living in a rental on the side of Schunemunk Mountain for one year when the pandemic hit. Lockdown left the pair feeling as though they'd missed out on the chance to get to know local queer people, and now they were stuck at home.

Describing their move to a rural area, Cyril said, "I feel like I'm a guest or somebody who's been invited into this space." This outlook helped them look past outward appearances for common ground or shared beliefs.

Their Orange County neighbors were Libertarians. The live-and-let-live philosophy meant Trump signs in election years, but it also meant the queer couple enjoyed freedom to be themselves. They flew a Pride flag year round and no one bothered them. When Marcel decided to apply for a pistol permit, a neighbor provided references and introduced them to other neighbors. As gardening had for me, gun culture was an entry point into community.

I couldn't help but view support for Trump as a direct threat to my existence and that of friends who were BIPOC, female, or lacked citizenship papers. Living on the margins compelled me to protect and shelter other marginalized people, to do what I could to make progress on the systemic issues that concentrated power in the hands of a few white men. Marcel and Cyril's acceptance of their Trump-loving, gun-toting neighbors stayed with me.

It wasn't so long ago that the queer community asked for, then demanded, tolerance and acceptance and finally love from those who saw us as shameful.

I benefited from grace extended toward earlier generations of gay people. If I could work toward extending grace to those whose opinions and beliefs did not map neatly onto mine, what immovable obstacles might shift and change?

Was it actually queer to love your neighbor as yourself?

Radical Hospitality

My own queer community came full circle in 2021, when I met Amy at a friend's birthday party. The lesbian neighbors she mentioned in our interview turned out to be our friends.

In our interview, Amy had been talkative and thoughtful. At the dinner party, she came alive like a sunflower turning toward the sun's warmth. Queer community was healing her wounds of not being held in the ways she had needed.

Queer people might choose different labels or pronouns, we might have different experiences and intersectional identities, but we were part of a massive family. We had each other's backs. We shared histories, slang, and ways of navigating the world.

We could be dismissive and catty and cruel to one another. It hurt more when insults came from those 'like us.' Queer community wasn't perfect, but we were always striving to do better by each other. We kept showing up. We would not quit us.

In high school, I'd been the weird, bookish kid who couldn't wait to escape to college. On campus, I gazed around the quad one late fall afternoon of freshman year, a realization sinking in. My fellow students were all bookish and weird. None of us had fit in where we came from, but here, we had found our fit. We belonged to Vassar and to one another.

As quickly as it came on, my unity vision left. I fell back into the rhythm of college life.

Now, I recalled that day on the quad with longing. I'd gotten it right, and I hadn't been ready for what interconnectedness suggested. I'd never been a joiner, never wanted to fit in or be mainstream, but in late 2021, I wanted to cross boundaries and ideological divides and touch a shared experience. This felt like the most queer thing to want, a test of ideals in an era when our species' survival depended on getting in right relationship.

Ann Marie, a lesbian living in Accord, embodied this generosity of spirit. When Ann Marie was a child, her family moved from Queens to the Hudson Valley where they homesteaded in an old Jewish bungalow colony with other Irish families.

She first started taking her wife upstate in 2000. They hosted concerts on their land and had friends camp out. When the bungalow began to feel crowded, in 2017, Ann Marie built a three-bedroom home with a ramp that allowed friends with wheelchairs to enter and exit the house independently.

Like her father before her, Ann Marie grew a little bit of everything: potatoes, peas, pumpkins, peppers, tomatoes, strawberries. She kept chickens, something she'd wanted to do since she was a child watching her Peruvian neighbors raise city chickens.

Every fall, when the harvest was complete, Ann Marie hosted a potluck. The shared meal took place around a brightly painted secondhand table, which she planned to donate at the end of the season. "Everything is something somebody created, whether it's their bread, or they made the pasta, or they made their own sauce from the tomatoes they grew or it's a pumpkin pie, or strawberries or jam," Ann Marie said, describing the get-together. "The only rule is no politics."

Ann Marie's table struck me as a queer sort of family, one without rules or bloodlines to dictate who was included and who was left out. One with room for all. Barring politics created a safe space where people could set aside partisan differences and see one another. Her radical hospitality strove to be more generous, more giving, to seek unity by coming together in spite of our differences.

This moved and triggered me.

What I knew of hospitality came from restaurant and catering work, where good service was inseparable from low wages that kept me financially insecure throughout my twenties. My hospitality skills came from my father's conditional love, which made me a quick study of expectations and ways to meet them.

In a blended family that left me guessing at my place, people-pleasing had been a survival skill. As an adult, I didn't want to put others' needs before my own. I admired radical hospitality, desired it for myself and my community, but could not trust I was welcome at the table.

Ann Marie's radical hospitality made me think of Chessie, too. As long as I reduced her to a single story, I could not see her. When my mental image of her shifted, she became a real, complex person. I would never know her, but my curiosity brought us closer. I moved from a distant sort of pity to kindness, then toward a form of love for her.

It wasn't a coincidence that this happened while I deepened my relationship with the land. With my hands in the earth, I could feel Chessie stretching toward me. I could feel the web of connections between my journey and queer history, between the land I cared for and the animals who sought shelter and food amid the shade of the black walnut trees.

All my life, I had been acutely aware of the differences between me and others. Queerness gave me a language to describe, then celebrate, those differences. Queer ancestors taught me where we had come from and who I might be. I'd thought of queer community as something out there: a gayborhood, a bar, a hideaway to be revealed after a lengthy search, a place where we could come and go as needed.

Queer homesteading connected me to a place and its people. It gave me a surrogate family and strengthened relationships with the non-human universe and my own ancestors.

Coming home, queerly, wasn't about gayborhoods or women's land or any other lost space that had once sheltered us. It was about anchoring into the source of our aliveness and giving from this generosity to those in need—not out of obligation, but from a desire to share, to be open, to bring that better world a bit closer to ours. Imperfect and full of joy, it could never be erased.

With Thanks

This book began as an oral history project, supported by funds from the Statewide Community Regrants Program, a regrant program of the New York State Council on the Arts with the support of the Office of the Governor and the New York State Legislature and administered by Arts Mid-Hudson. Thank you to Arts Mid-Hudson for supporting this project and the work of marginalized artists more broadly.

Many thanks to the people who volunteered to share their experiences of rural queer life with me for that project, whose words are excerpted within these pages. Your stories inspired me, challenged me, and helped to ground me in hope. I am grateful for your words, and your trust in me.

Transcripts of the full conversations are archived on my website, www.lindseydanis.com, if you wish to dive deeper.

The History Project, Boston's LGBTQ+ archive, sparked so much curiosity. Thank you for shepherding a piece of queer history, letting me have a peek, and preserving queer legacies from erasure.

Writer friends Adrienne Robillard, Gwenyth Reitz, and Wendra Colleen were early readers of these pages and helped shape the final version. Thank you for the careful edits, long conversations and support over the years.

Thank you to Portia Apple Melita who designed the cover image, originally used to promote this project and to Liliana Stinson, for help in launching this book you now read.

Finally, Aliza: thank you for building and sharing a life with me!

Lindsey Danis is a writer and LGBTQ+ travel expert whose work focuses on the intersection of identity and experience.

Lindsey's forthcoming book, *(Out) On the Road: The Radical Joy of Queer Travel,* teaches LGBTQ+ travelers how to navigate the world with ease, confidence, and joy. It will be published in 2026.

Lindsey's writing has been recognized in *Best American Travel Writing* and anthologized in *The Best New True Crime Stories, Nourishing Resistance: Stories of Food, Protest, and Mutual Aid,* and *No Contact: Writers on Family Estrangement.* Short pieces have appeared in *AFAR, Fodor's, Condé Nast Traveler, Longreads,* and *Eater* among others.

Lindsey has a BA in English from Vassar College and an MFA in Creative Writing from Emerson College, and has received fellowships and support from Stone Soup Community Press, Alderworks Alaska, Limnisa, Murphy Writing, the Virginia G. Piper Center for Creative Writing at Arizona State University, Sundress Academy for the Arts, and New York State Council on the Arts.

Originally from Boston, Lindsey now lives in the Hudson Valley, where she often cooks, hikes, and kayaks. Follow Lindsey's adventures near and far on Instagram: @lindsey.danis.writer

www.ingramcontent.com/pod-product-compliance
Lightning Source LLC
LaVergne TN
LVHW090542110826
845146LV00003B/1228
* 9 7 9 8 8 9 9 9 0 4 1 9 6 *